T0159190

TALES *OF THE* LOO

MD John

PARTRIDGE

To order additional copies of this book, contact
Toll Free +65 3165 7531 (Singapore)
Toll Free +60 3 3099 4412 (Malaysia)
orders.singapore@partridgepublishing.com

www.partridgepublishing.com/singapore

CONTENTS

Acknowledgements...vii

Flat Based Encounter 1
Shit Hole Genius... 7
The Night Soil Man 21
Seladang's Dung of Challenge – The Power of Fart 27
Jungle "Jamban" Guest 38
Son's POP-up Ordeal 48
Wind Break-A-Loo – The Medan Dip 55
Cling Clang – Fire in the Hole 72
Breakneck Discharge... 84
Month End Feast 89

ACKNOWLEDGEMENTS

Writing this compilation of short stories would never have taken off if not for my family's continuous pestering. They were full of confidence that my book would one day be a best seller if only I would start writing or just to put my thoughts on paper. That was close to seven years ago. Each time I was at Starbucks Bangsar, out came my laptop and with a mug of hot Americano, I started tapping away under the watchful eyes of my wife Jane, keeping me company. At times accompanied by my daughter Heera, and son Hamish, sharing their thoughts and giggling whenever I asked them for their views after a few sentences. Thank you to the one thing I did totally right in my life; my family.

Thank you Jane, for being the editor and to have gone through the grammar, spelling, sentence structures and punctuation marks. What an eye opener. So glad I married an English teacher! You opened up a whole new world of the English language which I had taken for granted or which I thought I knew. Rewording, rewriting and deleting unnecessary "ands", "buts" and extremely long sentences practically making up a whole paragraph, that will make a difference in how this book will be read.

Heera, finding the time to patiently sit and help me rethink what life is all about. One can write about the foulest things that come with the call of Nature. But in your funny, sarcastic and uncompromising attitude you made it sound and feel so very accommodating and ridiculously funny. Thank you for being this wonderful child I call my own.

The book was ready many months ago but my attempts to locate a reasonable publisher was a big question mark. Cost was another factor to be considered. Thank you Hamish, for sourcing for me the Partridge Publishing and to extend your "temporary loan with interest" when I thought that this book was never going to hit the market. An irritating but wonderful son any father would be proud of.

Should I or should I not have illustrations included in my book? What about the front cover depicting my thoughts and words that make up this book? For this, I have to thank my lucky stars and of course Hamish, and through his good friend, Michelle; they got my illustrator, Will Win Yang. An illustrator who patiently listened to my thoughts and words and came up with the most hilarious pieces that depicted summarily what each story was about. A person who never considered dollars and cents but passion to her interest in

Art. A definite partner in my future tales; be prepared for more of *Willwin Yang* Artwork in the near future.

And many of my friends, near and far, (including those who have passed on), who in one way or another, encouraged me and always told me, *"Just waiting to buy your book."* **THANK YOU.**

Jane, Hamish & Heera
Always

FLAT BASED ENCOUNTER

Him: "Aiyoo, can you not drive any faster? Why is it every time I need to go to the toilet, you drive the car taking your own sweet time?"

Her: "Shut-up la. Now you know how it feels when I have a tummy upset. You are no different."

Him: "Okay, okay, stop the car at the lobby entrance and you go park. Give me the room keys. Already coming out; quick la."

Her: "Kids, follow Papa."

Him: "No need, just stop the damn car. Oh God, cannot stand anymore!"

Her: "Eat la like a pig; serves you right. Follow Papa so that you can open the room door for me once I have parked the car."

The car door is flung open and Papa dashes out of the car, followed closely by his kids holding their noses. They try not to hear Papa's foul language as he tries to elegantly do a quick march to the lift. Son advises that he use the hotel toilet next to the reception but as always, Papa's bowels never open willingly to foreign and alien loos. It took Papa quite a while to adjust his bums to the one in the hotel room and for Papa; comfort in the loo is everything, even if it means he has to run up the stairs to the sixth floor in case the lift is down. Thank God the lift is open, ready to receive the already slowly wheezing puff of coagulated, putrefied wind seeping out through the cotton pants, now drenched in sweat.

Once at their floor, Papa quickly foxtrots to the door and opens it, dashing, spearheading towards the toilet. Kids following a safe distance behind, avoiding the sting of the back blast of the now almost uncontrollable stench wheezing out. They see pants, then undies, getting airborne and hear the toilet door slam shut followed by silence.

Once inside, Papa switches on the toilet switch but only darkness prevails. *"The kids may not have placed the key card into the slot for the lights to come on"* Papa thinks. Too dark to even see where the pot is located but Papa quickly pushes down the seat and lands his bums *flat* on the seat.

Surprisingly, Papa's bums do not experience the G force of gravity or the gripping curve of the seat around the bums. The bums experience a flat launching pad, and instead of a downward surge of Melaka's Baba Nyonya's exquisite cuisine (now a totally different recipe altogether), Papa instead feels a warm but (surprisingly) gentle and smooth, slimy, squashy ooze flowing down his legs. His bums feel like they are slipping each time he moves. What is happening? What is this? Instead of feeling a splurge of downward climax relieving him of his unwanted waste into the receiving bowl, he neither hears the sound of downward waste drops nor the pleasure of sudden comfort of an empty bowel. And that putrid, smell of liquified, ammonic diarrhea, slowly engulfing the whole room...... and then, there was light.... And there was also **SHIT**!!! ALL OVER!!!

Hell, it was just all over the floor, slithering downwards as contaminated lava, from an upside-down volcano. As such, instead of an upward eruption as would how and should a volcano spit, the "lava" was flowing off from a flattened plateau that evenly ensured not only the floor but the outer reaches of the whole bowl was totally covered with a technicolor of "you know what."

There was no stopping the flow and too late to lift the seat which incidentally made up the "plateau" where the mouth of the volcano was now precariously sitting on. Only then, Papa realized that in the dark, not only did he pull down the seat but the cover as well. No wonder the G force was absent. No wonder there was no hanging bottom. Papa had to slowly do a couple of slow bum lifts to allow the "mouth of the erupting volcano" release the now oozing liquid that practically flooded the floor of the toilet. First thought; *"how do I clean this mess of liquified, contaminated, ammonia smelling putrefying mass of lava (SHIT)."*

There was no toilet roll but thank God there was a bidet just next to a sink hole. But water alone, was not enough and Papa needed rags to clean this mess (oops sorry, SHIT). None available. Hotel towels were there but the question on Papa's mind was how to dispose of the towels after cleaning the human waste splurged all over the small cubicle.

Lifting the now wet and yucky pasted bum off the toilet cover, Papa tiptoed slowly, careful not to slip and fall as he moved towards the door. Opening it just enough to peep outside and see if anyone was near the toilet.

"Aiyoo Mummy, what's that stench? Papa, what are you depositing in the toilet? Now no one can use it."

"Need to teach that son some manners and consideration. My whole reputation will be flushed if he gets hold of the mess I "created" which I need to clean."

Tiptoeing back to where the bidet was, Papa surveys the *'shit-uation'* to plan the clean up. This is extremely critical since any wrong direction, speed and flow of the spray from the bidet may just cause a tidal wave of shit to be strewn all over the toilet wall. As such, Papa has to carefully use the spray just slightly above the floor, millimeters away from the yellowish, brown boils of slimy fluid and slowly press the 'trigger'.

Swoosh ... the 'cannon' fires a volley of spray and just as what Papa had feared, there was now lava on the wall sliding down. The ordeal of cleaning up the mess took a whole half hour and another half to have a bath. Cleaning the legs, arms and bums were okay, but Papa is definite there are 'some' lodged in the cavities of his body, never before ventured. For one, a lingering smell at his nose tips emitted from his manly moustache.

All done. As Papa comes out of the toilet, he sees his family peacefully watching The Discovery Channel. If only they knew of the ordeal and discovery he had gone through; would beat any adventure trek the channel had to offer. All that remained of the experience and "adventure" was a faint pungent and aromatic stench of Malacca's Baba Nyonya's special, that had been ejected from an upside down volcano with no escape bowl to receive it except a flat based white plateau.

Moral of the story......?

When there is light and you can see clearly, you do not have to waste unnecessary time cleaning after. Light gives one the opportunity to keep oneself and the surroundings always clean and in control. Never grope in the dark.

SHIT HOLE GENIUS

Shit holes, 40 – 50 years ago were not as high tech as now. What with the various bowls that are so elegantly shaped and, in some instances, to assimilate to the flesh temperature of the buttocks. This, so as to avoid unnecessary shock waves to evolve due to temperature variances between the bowels, rectum and room temperature. Even the squatting units allow ample space and very firm bases where one does not fear of accidentally slipping into the deep end of the ever-uninviting tunnel that leads to the cesspool comprising of unimaginable droppings deposited by all who use the comforts of the cubicle in executing nature's call. Basically, a comfort to be appreciated when one is indisposed in the toilet answering the call of nature....as the saying goes.... he or she is sitting [squatting] on their throne.

It was never like this in the early 50s (or even very much earlier). They had in those days what we used to refer to as the latrine or out-house which was situated at the rear of the house. One reason was to ensure anyone intending to do their business executed it as far away as possible from the rest of the family members or tenants. What more with the noxious smell the latrine used to emit; hovering around its location. Once in a while, a strong gust of wind would present to those in the home a whiff of jeypine and "protein" stored in those buckets that were part and parcel of the latrine's contents, tucked safely away in the backdrops of homes those days.

My father, a "dresser", or as they now refer to them as male nurses or hospital attendants, had his own clinic; the Eastern Medical Hall. His clinic was very similar to what most private practitioners have these days minus the sophisticated soft and hardware; thanks to the high-tech world of today.

And yes, there was a latrine. Nothing sophisticated but a simple bucket system where the remains that were excreted dropped into a bucket and its contents removed every late evening by the night soil carrier.

Note: For a more detailed description of the methodology used, read **"The Night Soil Man"**.

There were times however where the night soil carrier failed to remove the waste droppings and the day's deposit remained intact for another day or two. This attracted blue arsed flies, cockroaches, creepy crawlies (left to one's imagination) usually where the uninvited guests came to savour and nourish themselves with what the human waste had to offer.

Patients usually used this latrine, and in a day one could expect at least five to seven visiting the privy. No holds barred. Just go in there and *"lepas"* [let go]. The nurse employed by my father would regularly pour in *Jeypine* and a little soda powder to ensure the above crawlies were limited and the stench contained at a minimum. Yet, they came (crawlies and patients alike) and the stench stayed; immaterial how much effort was taken to limit the negativities that was emitted.

The clinic closed at four each evening and very seldom any patient would do a night visit. Most often, they would come directly to the house or my father used to do a night call visit to their homes if required. The hospital was there but some of the more regular patients still needed my father's soft and soothing touch from years of serving the sick.

And it was, one such night, that my father got a call from Choo Ah Chong. Yes, phones existed then but not what you get now-a-days. However, they played their role quite effectively. Anyway, the caller, Choo sounded very agitated and worried. His wife who was eight months pregnant was feeling extremely sick and felt it was time; though one month too early.

It was way past midnight and my father advised Choo to take her to the hospital. He would then meet him there. That was the most logical advice given, I presume. My father quickly got out of bed, woke up my mum (who incidentally was also in her sixth or seventh month with you know who in her womb), and told her about Choo's wife. All were close friends. What more could you expect from a small town like Tangkak where a fart 30 houses away could be traced to the owner? All the same, my mum too was up in a jiffy and got ready herself. She also went to wake up the nurse, Julie Yap (who was also known as Missy) who stayed in our house as well.

"Missy, it is Choo's wife. Going to deliver. John and I will be meeting her in the hospital. Watch over the kids."

My family lived along Jalan Sialang (Sialang Road) and the hospital was along Jalan Payamas (Payamas Road). Choo, who dealt with household goods, lived on the top floor of his shop lot; also along Jalan Payamas. My father's clinic was situated along Sialang Road itself. To go to the hospital, my father had to pass the clinic, come to a crossroads and take a left, where the hospital was approximately 4 miles away. All in all, a quick drive.

Once both my parents were in the Austin, they headed towards the hospital. As they were approaching the clinic, my mum noticed a car with its headlights brightly beaming, parked by the side of the road.

"John, looks like Choo's car. What is it doing here? Thought you told him to meet us at the hospital?" my mother enquired.

My father (a man of few words) did not say anything but slowly parked his car just behind Choo's and got out.

"Choo, apa pasal awak tunggu sini? Saya suruh pergi hospital cepat-cepat." (Choo, why are you waiting here? I told you to go to the hospital quickly).

"Doktor [though only a dresser, the townsfolk always referred to my father as "doctor"], *saya punya beni lagi selamat sini. Sana takut. Sini sudah biasa. Doktor tengok la cepat. Saya banyak risau. Dia dalam kereta."* (Doctor, my wife is safer here. There, scared. Used to being here. Doctor, attend to her quickly. I am very worried. She is in the car).

My father went to the back seat and did a quick examination. He quickly then went to his car, took out the keys to the clinic and opened the locks on the detachable door planks. With the help of Choo, both removed the planks that were used in the old days as a barrier into the shop and told Choo to bring his wife into the clinic. Choo's neighbour, Nancy, who was sitting in the back seat with his wife, assisted to take his wife in the clinic.

"Perlahan-lahan. Jaga," (slowly. Careful) my mother reminded as the three of them assisted Mrs. Choo into the

clinic. In the meantime, my father had already prepared his patient's examination room where he used to conduct minor surgeries; and now most probably to deliver a baby. He was very aware that there was no turning back and that the baby, though one month too early was already due as he had observed that her water bag had already broken when he did a quick examination of her in the car.

Slowly aided by the three, Mrs. Choo walked through the clinic's main door but before being ushered into the surgery room, requested to use the latrine. This request was immediately denied by my mother because it would not be advisable especially since she was on the verge of delivery. She then requested to sit down just outside the examination room and my mum went into the room to check on my father and see if he needed any assistance.

My mum was out of sight for not more than ten minutes when apparently Mrs. Choo practically demanded that her husband take her to the latrine. No amount of persuasion from either Choo or Nancy could stop her demands. As the saying goes "never upset a woman about to experience labour". And to the latrine they went.

When my mum came out to get Mrs. Choo, none of them was anywhere to be seen. Then suddenly a piercing cry was heard from the rear of the clinic and my mum knew that the idiot of a woman had gone to the latrine assisted by another two nincompoops (sorry for the harsh word) as well. Not good at all.

"John, she has gone to the latrine. Come quickly!" my mum yelled for my father to come quickly to the rear latrine. When my mum arrived at the latrine, she had the shock of her life. Choo was in the latrine trying to hold his wife who was screaming and seemed totally uncontrollable. Nancy was standing nearby and practically shivering.

"Aunty, the baby come out already. Now in the "jamban" (toilet bucket). *Aiyoo, all the tahi (shit) inside the jamban, cover the baby. Hidup tak tahu (whether alive, do not know). So "busuk" (smelly)."*

"Aiyoooo mana doctor? Anak saya dalam jamban. Tolong la, tolong. Tak berani angkat, masih lekat hooo. Tolong!!!" (where is doctor? My child is in the toilet bucket. Help, help. I don't dare lift, still attached [referring to the umbilical cord]) shrieked Choo. *"Mati lo"* (Die).

"Diam" (Quiet), my father yelled as he approached the chaos. *"Choo, lu keluar dari tandas. Biar saya uruskan. Jangan takut. Saya ada sini,"* (Choo, you get out of the latrine. Let me handle. Do not be afraid. I am here), my father instructed assuring that all will be well.

In the meantime, my mum, who herself was quite shocked not knowing what to do next, but having full confidence in my father, stood by waiting for his instructions.

"Esther" (my mum's maiden name), *get me the surgical scissors from the dish and towels."*

To be noted here, my father spoke to my mother only in Tamil, so as not to alarm Choo.

My mum rushed to the examination room in double quick time. She understood my father's instructions quite well; as she had in the past assisted him quite regularly.

"And bring the torchlight as well," he yelled after her.

"Nancy, bawa air dari dapur. Ada yang sudah masak dekat itu almari pinggan." (Nancy, bring water from the kitchen. There is water that has been boiled near the cutlery cupboard). Nancy went quickly though still quite shaken from what she had observed. In her mind, the baby was dead. What a shitty way to go.

Choo was a goner. Not knowing exactly what to do. But he looked at my father and knew that if the baby was alive, he could depend on "Dr. John" to save the child and his wife; who herself had almost lost consciousness.

The light bulb in the latrine was quite dim and my father found it quite difficult to fully gauge the situation. But once my mum arrived, he quickly grabbed the torchlight and assessed the scenario before his eyes. Though Mrs. Choo was perspiring profusely, she seemed okay but tensed. What can one expect after having shat (opps!, delivered), her baby into the shit pot. The only thing on her mind at that moment was, *"how am I going to wash the shit out of this fella?"* This based on conversation with my mum long after Mrs. Choo's ordeal was over.

"Here, hold the torchlight and focus it where you can see the umbilical cord. I am going to cut it. Call Choo," were my father's instructions to my mum.

"Choo, cepat mari. You bangun la. Jangan duduk macam sudah mati. Cepat!," (Choo, come quickly. Get up. Do not sit down like you are dead. Quick!), my mum called out to Choo.

"Apa you mau lagi? Itu anak macam mana mahu angkat? Sudah jadi tahi. Macam mana mahu angkat? Tak berani!" (What more do you want? How to carry the baby? Already became shit. How to carry? Not brave), cried Choo. His voice full of concern and fear for both his wife and his baby in the shit pot.

"Hoi Choo. You mari ambil you punya beni keluar dari tandas. Itu anak baik. Saya jaga. Jangan takut." (Hey Choo. You come and take your wife out of the latrine. The child is okay.

I will take care of the baby. Do not be afraid), my father assured Choo as he tied the umbilical cord at two ends and snapped cut the center between the knots.

My father's assuring words pacified Choo who very quickly went near the latrine door and slowly guided his wife out of the cubicle. Surprisingly, other than the slimy birth fluids, she escaped the shitty mess her baby was currently in. The moment she stepped out on clean ground aided by Choo, suddenly, all heard the sound of a tight whack and then the ever piercing, gurgling wail of a new born baby taking in air and all that shit, announcing its arrival into this world.

"*Waa Choo, u dapat anak laki*" (Waa Choo, you got a boy). Choo gave a shitty smile and his wife breathed a sigh of relief.

My father later narrated the experience whereby when he had gone into the latrine (the cubicle which was extremely small), he studied the situation and knew that he had to act fast; if not the baby would have choked to death; what with two days of uncollected human faeces still floating in the bucket. Time was of essence as he quickly but meticulously knotted two ends of the umbilical cord and cut with the sterilised scissors my mother had handed over to him. It was apparently quite tricky as the baby was already emerced in the bucket full of shit and he had to control himself from puking due to the stench and slime all over his hands right up to his elbows.

Once the cord was cut and Choo had guided his wife out of the cubicle, my father had to gently lift the baby out of the bucket and carefully but firmly hold the baby exposing its slimy buttocks for the ever famous "whack of life" for it to experience its first breath of "fresh" air into its lungs for the very first time. In this case, shit included but in small specks and doses.

The baby was quickly placed on the clean towels which my mum had brought and with the water which Nancy had ready, the shit was wiped clean and this took quite a bit of time to achieve. For the next few weeks Choo Liow laughed and gurgled his way into everyone's hearts. He was bathed in practically different perfumed shampoos and patted with Lavender and Johnson's baby powder but it was a long time before friends and relatives were wanting to cradle him for long periods. Maximum they would fondle and play with the baby was no more than ten minutes; maybe less. They always whispered about a strange odour that the child seemed to emit. But that only lasted for a month or so.

No one knew about what had actually happened; how this beautiful baby came via being practically dropped from the womb right into the shit bucket way past midnight in Eastern Medical Hall and rescued by my father.

Choo however, relieved that his wife and newborn son were ok, built a very close rapport with my father and at times used to convey to him his concerns if this child would make it big in this ever suspicious world.

"Lahir dalam tahi; mana bolih jadi pandai? Kesihan dia." (Born in shit; can he ever be clever? Poor boy) he used to lament. My father used to console him and assure him that God usually had strange ways and best to trust the One above.

It was a well-kept secret which no one knew other than the five who witnessed this strange delivery that night. Incidentally, I was born a few months after Choo Liow and it was many years after that when I had already left school when my mum one day told me what had happened.

One late morning when I was sitting on the steps with my mum chatting away, my neighbour, Ah Soe, came over to join us.

"*Waa, itu anak Choo banyak pandai. Belajar tinggi. Sekarang jadi doctor besar di Amerika. Cepat dia naik. Ada orang kata dia kecil makan tahi. Tahi apa tak tahu*" (Wow, that Choo's son is really very clever. Very highly educated. Now he is a well-known doctor in America. He has progressed very fast. Some say when he was young, he used to eat shit. Wonder what kind of shit it was). Nancy, by the way was her niece.

After Ah Soe left, my mum told me the whole story. And yes, Choo Liow was an outstanding student in school. Many a time when he used to beat me flat in acquiring very high marks, my late father, (God rest his soul) used to tell me to sip his urine if I wanted to excel like him.

Not only in school did he excel but also in the outside world. Guess he had a taste of the kind of shit this world was going to offer him and I suppose he was prepared. And not only him. In later years, even his sons followed in his footsteps. Not that they too were delivered in a shit pot but excelled in their studies as well. Guess the bucket in which their father dropped into was actually the pot of gold at the end of a rainbow.

Guess his father's fears were unfounded. As from its own ashes, a Phoenix rises, reborn once again in all its splendour and elegance, maybe, just maybe so too Choo Liow. As he was delivered into a bucket where no man would dare to venture, Choo Liow was destined to be raised (picked up, more like it) from the valley of shit and immaculately transformed into a genius with far reaching achievements adorned with gold and silver.

Moral of the Story........

Immaterial our roots and where we emerged from, many may pass judgement pertaining to our background and poor upbringing. At the end of the day, as what the poet Robert Frost penned, choosing the road less travelled will ultimately make a whole lot of difference.

THE NIGHT SOIL MAN

During the early 50s and 60s, many households did not have the kind of toilets we have nowadays. The elegant state of the art bowls that come with bidets of various kinds including ones that actually shoot a spray of water where it matters most and every little deposit is so very easily flushed just by the push of a button or pulling down the flush handle. And in a jiffy and a swirl such as a mini whirlpool, every little bit is totally flushed off to an underground sewage tank.

When I was young, this was not the case. We had toilets that were usually located behind our house; lone and away from "civilization" where especially at nights one had to walk even during thunderstorms just to do a quick deposit after a hearty meal.

In some homes, the toilet was located within the house but very often than not, at the back. Where I used to stay, which used to be my father's medical clinic, a shop lot, such toilets usually faced the back lane. As such, there were rows of shoplots on both sides, and each had a small square opening at the bottom where the toilet was situated. If one were bold enough and covered one's nostrils or placing the *"chap kapak"* ointment at the tip of the nose to ward off the stench and brush off the large smelly "blue arsed flies" swarming around the vicinity, you could flip open the side covering and notice the existence of a rusty bucket with a curved handle (like a pail) sitting squarely on the floor of the small cubicle considered as the toilet. Very often, when the flip of the covering is open, other than the stench, one could also get a faint smell of Jeypine. Do not ask me why anyone would want to open the side covering to examine the bucket but sometimes at that age, it is quite difficult to overcome curiosity; immaterial if it kills the cat.

As the latrines come minus the flush system, the task and responsibility of removing the deposits, rested squarely on the shoulders of the **Night Soil Man** or as they used to call him those days, *"the jamban cleaner"* literally meaning the toilet cleaner.

The *"jamban cleaner"* (bare-bodied, wearing only a dark blue coloured boxers, used to be known as the Chinaman underwear and a pair of Japanese slippers on his feet) had, as part of his cleaning tools, a long bamboo pole with two old and rusty pails hanging from either end. One had some water mixed with the Jeypine solution (water which he will from time to time request from households he visits during his mission of collecting their deposits). The other pail (without a cover), filled with only the choicest identified waste which he carefully "selects". Once he has done the collection of the best waste, he will splash water into the latrine pot and with another of his tools, an old and short "lidi" broom ("lidi" as from the coconut leaf "backbone" clumped together to make brooms), he will quickly wash the remnants of the waste inside the latrine pot and throw them into the "longkang" (drain) running parallel along the shoplots where the latrines were situated. And I remember, those were the very "longkangs" where my friends and I (sometimes accompanied by my sister), usually after school in the afternoons, got together to catch "ikan sepat" (a kind of drain fish) and tadpoles. Many times however, I used to wonder what he did with the remnants in the other pail where he kept the carefully scooped deposits; and where exactly he disposed of them. Only later I came to know where those deposits ultimately ended up.

At times, some of the more mischievous boys in the neighborhood used to follow Ah Seng (that was his name), and taunt him by calling him silly names, making him quite angry at times. And his only weapon in warding off these urchins was to dip his short "lidi" broom into the bucket of scooped deposits and fling it at the boys who ran helter skelter trying to avoid the droplets of slimy ooze shooting off from the tip of the broom towards them. Some were not so lucky; going home smelling of you know what and

usually ended up getting a thrashing from their parents;
their fathers in particular. In that way, Ah Seng did get his
revenge.

And yes; what did happen to the deposits collected
carefully by Ah Seng in the other pail? Be prepared to
accept the truth and reality of the matter.

My father was a "dresser". This was what hospital assistants
were known as those days. I guess because they usually

dressed wounds and sores, especially sores with puss and yellowish blood (and at time slimy looking worms easing their way out of badly infested pores on the legs and arms of the patient). One of my father's regular patients was Ah Seng. He never used to visit my father in the clinic but used to come in the evenings, off and on to have his wounds and sores cleaned and dressed. My father never charged him and most often than not had the best of conversations about you know what.

It was during one of these visits, with Ah Seng squatting next to my father, with a shirt on and his usual Chinaman's blue underwear, as my father was inspecting his sores and wounds that I came to know of where the deposits from the other pail went to. The conversation went something like this which nearly made me puke to glory:

"*Loclo ah* (he used to refer to my father as "*loclo*" or doctor though my father was not one but Ah Seng's way of showing respect), *waa...gua punya kaki banyak teluk. Selalu nana keluar, bau busuk. Ini kerja ambik tahi lak bagus. Lak sihat. Lagi pun itu tahi saya hantar kebun sayur. Lia olang lak bayarr banyak. Tapi itu sayur pakai saya punya tahi saya pilih yang bagus. Itu sayur sawi jual pasar banyak hilau. Saya nampak loklo selalu beli. Baguslak?*" ("Doctor", my legs are really bad. Always oozing with bad smelling puss. Collecting shit is really bad business. Moreover, the shit which I carefully choose to send to the vegetable farm as fertilizer, they do not pay me well. But the vegetables using my shit are good and very green. Many times I have seen you in the market buying those vegetables. Really good, right?). My father nodded in full agreement. It was a long, long time before I ever ate "sawi" or any other vegetable again. But come to think of it, it did taste quite good; out of the ordinary, if I might say so myself.

Moral of the Story......

What goes round comes around. What we dispose of today will come back to us in one way or the other. Just like in the movie, "The Lion King", where Mufasa educates his son, Simba, on The Circle of Life. So please do be careful of what you say or do which can cause repercussions, either having positive or negative consequences.

SELADANG'S DUNG OF CHALLENGE - THE POWER OF FART

As young officers, we were required to undergo intensive jungle warfare operations in some of the most remote and treacherous terrains in the country. And so it was that during one such exercise, we were air-dropped via a Nuri Helicopter in a remote part of the Kedah jungles somewhere close to the Malaysia-Thai border, located very near an area known as *Padang Lembu* (Cow's Field). We comprised of a Platoon strength of about 40, and as soon as we hit solid ground, we immediately went into our standard operation drill of securing the perimeter; ensuring that prior to setting up camp all possible entry points into our campsite were well secured and safe. Securing and setting up our base took quite a bit of the morning whilst lunch was prepared by our platoon cook, Private Salleh.

We took a breather around noon and sat down for a well-deserved meal of rice, spicy mutton curry, green peas, jungle *"ulam"* (raw greens), *"chilli padi"* (bird's eye chilly) and *"belacan"* [fermented prawn paste that gives a kick to both the taste of simple food as well as to one's bowels if taken on a hot sweaty day].

Once lunch was over, the boys continued with the usual settling down in a jungle camp whilst the late Lt. Hassan Che Pak (may his soul rest in peace) and I lay on our hammocks under some shades; black coffee and a Benson between our lips. A good smoke, and thick black coffee, *kaw-kaw* (local slang expressing satisfaction guaranteed), to the taste was all we needed after such a good, hearty jungle meal.

Both Hassan and I were quietly chatting when we started feeling a bit uneasy and felt a churning sensation slowly but surely brewing from within. Maybe it was because we had just too much *"chilli padi"* or the spicy *"belacan"* and spicy mutton curry but its effect was slowly taking its toll in our already hot tummies. I could see sweat slowly trickling down Hassan's neck and as for me, I started sweating profusely as well and knew that I could not just lie on my hammock expecting the tide to go away. It was hot and the fear of even breaking wind in case it released more than just wind was an option I did not want to consider.

"Tak tahan la. Kena labur," (Cannot hold on. Need to deposit – as one deposits money in a bank) quipped Hassan.

"Tapi tandas belum siap. Masih gali lubang," (But the latrine is not completed as yet. Still being dug) I informed Hassan. The boys who were enlisted to do the latrine were still at it and needed time for it to be completed and ready to receive deposits.

"Tak tahan la. Kena lepas. Jom cari tempat 'air drop'." (Come on. Let us look for a place to 'air drop' – a term used to describe releasing one's bowels not in a latrine, but any ground with a hole dug for the business to be concluded.)

"Ok la. Saya pun dah tak larat tahan." (Ok. I too cannot hold on any longer.) I jumped off my hammock agreeing with Hassan to look for a suitable and secluded clearing to do our business.

With our water bottles and army regulation spades, we took off through the thick undergrowth towards a small stream which we had earlier identified when we had done the initial recce just before setting up camp. It was approximately a hundred odd meters from where we were based and though generally "safe" we still moved with extreme caution; our eyes darting, covering all angles to ensure we did not encounter any unexpected and unwelcomed *"penyamun"* (bandits), who seemed to frequent this area we were currently based at. We were a few kilometres from the location where a new university was currently being constructed.

As we neared the stream, the sound of its cool running water could be heard but more so, a very strong stench of buffalo dung or droppings could be sensed prodding our nostrils. We knew that this area was quite often frequented by animals, especially elephants and water buffaloes, but they were not much of a threat as they came out only in the early mornings for a dip in the stream and to quench their thirst. Even if they did emerge, we would have heard them quite easily as animals tend to make quite a ruckus to warn anything nearby to stay clear as they were going to use the place for their own; or so we thought.

When we reached the stream, we noticed that it was quite fast flowing with soft sand on either side of its banks. The bank across the stream consisted of thick undergrowth which was quite evident with very few pathways that were visible. We both went in opposite directions, a short distance from each other and chose spots that we felt comfortable and dug holes with our spades for the intended 'air drops' we were about to execute shortly. In the meantime, we placed our M16s against a small shrub, ignoring one of the basic principles of weapon SOPs (Standard Operation Procedures) and that was never place your personal weapon more than an arm's length away as we may never know when we would require to use it at lightning speed. In this case, our M16s were about three feet away from where we were squatting and the only items we were holding were our water bottles, where we needed the water to wash our butts once our business was complete.

Once the holes were dug, no time was wasted as we quickly dropped our pants and with both legs firmly on either side of the hole, we relieved ourselves with one quick burst of liquid shit, the smell of which overpowered any dung that was around the area, emitting at that very instant a pungent odour of *belacan*, mutton and peas; sweet to our own personal senses but a catastrophe to another

We were both chatting away, again a fool-hardy thing to do.... may-be both of us were *"pukau-ed"* (possessed by jungle spirits) as we were practically doing all the wrong things –contrary to what we had been taught. All of a sudden we heard a rustling noise from the other side of the stream; a good ten meters away from where we were squatting. We were already in the process of having dropped a few pieces of remnants after the initial burst of liquified waste and the sudden rustling opposite from where we were squatting, caught us by surprise; shock to be more precise. A quick look to where we had placed our M16s and at the same instance, an attempt to wash our bottoms with water did not materialise as without any warning (other than the rustling of bushes), out of nowhere this massive hulk of a giant, with penetrating curved horns; the tip of which I swear were sharp as a Masai's spear, came rushing out into the open and just stopped short at the edge of the river in front of us; thank God it was on the other side.

The **gaur**, also called **Indian bison**,
or **Seladang** in Malaysia,
is the largest extant bovine, native to South Asia and
Southeast Asia. It is a strong and massively built species
and considered among the largest living
land animals. Source: Wikipedia

As we continued squatting not daring to even move a
muscle, the massive bull, though ten meters away, looked
like a whole mountain staring down upon us. Its head was
rolling from side to side exhibiting its greyish white horns
in the most threatening gesture wanting to pierce its razor
sharp tips into whatever that was in its way. Our fear was
that it might just run across the stream and gore the life out
of us.... abdomen, shit and all; and we knew that we would
not stand a chance against this giant. Our pants were still

wrapped just below our knees making it impossible for us to get up quickly to get our M16s for protection; not that the bullets would have made a difference. So all we could do was to control ourselves from shaking too much and pray that the **Seladang** (that's what it was) would turn around and trot back to wherever it appeared from. Strangely, the best part was we continued doing our business but felt a bit slimy along our thighs. Only later we realised that when we first saw this bull appear, we had tried to get up whilst the purge was still flowing out and must have splashed on our thighs and legs; not that it mattered at all during this tense encounter with Mr. Seladang.

By now the bull was getting totally agitated. Its nostrils were fiercely emitting misty mucus and foaming at the mouth whilst scrapping the ground with its muscular hooves, as if waiting for the right opportune moment to launch itself from where it was, and onto us. That bull must have weighed more than a ton from our estimates!

Then, as if it caught a whiff of odour alien to its nostrils, the bull started to trot back and forth, all the time lifting its head to smell the stink; something totally pungent which the wind was taking from where we were stuck towards the opposite end of the stream. From the look on the bull's face, it was not too amused that its own dung pong was being overpowered by this reeking smell; though to us it was sweet perfume. The anger gleamed in its eyes and its hoofs started digging faster, harder, deeper and more aggressively and felt totally annoyed as the stench of our waste and the sound of an uncontrollable fart that would have silenced a GPMG (General Purpose Machine Gun), brought to where it was by the wind that had suddenly altered its course towards this jungle Mike Tyson, the champion boxer.

One's fart has always been heaven to one's own nostrils but a total disgust to another, often being cursed to glory by the one having to bear its unbearable aroma. So too I guess it was with Mr. Seladang, when the putrefied stench of both our farts coupled with the decomposed smell of diarrhoea that we had just released, hit its nostrils. It practically went berserk. If one's fart could spell hell for another, never could I imagine the impact it could have on a wild jungle animal that was used to only smelling and being intoxicated by the smell of its own dung. We were expecting it to charge at us like all fury let loose, but instead, it was the complete opposite. Its tail suddenly shot straight up towards heaven as if requesting for holy intervention to get it out of this scenario it was currently facing (smelling to be more exact).

Then with a swirling of its massive frame, looked more like a sudden shiver, the beast turned around and our hearts did a quick jerk of relief when we saw its butt now facing us as it started to slowly trot back to where it had emerged from. Then, right before our eyes, the most impossible of impossibilities happened. With its tail now in an upright vertical position, we saw with our naked eyes a massively huge "log" of dung (the colour of which looked very similar to what Christmas Turkeys are stuffed with - those purchased from hotels and supermarkets), slowly being squeezed out from the bull's sphincter and a never-ending drop to the ground, the length of which I can never imagine or believe, to this very day. We just stared in awe, when without a moment's hesitation, the bull turned its head around and with a speed you can never fathom, whack the shit out of the dung with its horns of steel, even before it could hit the ground! Like scattered pieces of rock from an exploding oncoming meteor, the dung just speared the ten meters across the stream directly towards where we were squatted dump struck. Even before we could utter *"Oh Shit!"* we were splashed with hot and sticky green paste all over us....and we scrammed. No invitation needed for that!

We practically crawled from where we were, and in the process, dragging from the holes we had dug, our own poo with our pants clinging around our knees as we grabbed our M16s and scrambled for our lives towards base. We decided to take a dip in another nearby waterhole to clear the mess we were covered in. One cannot expect two Royal Commissioned Officers to walk into camp, drenched in human and bull excreta in front of their men, and tell this tale. Till this day and until now....no one knew except Hassan (and he is dead and gone...rest his soul), of our episode with Malaysia's mammoth beast, the *Seladang.*

Now, that is the power of FART.

Note: We came back two days later as we had left our water bottles when we scrambled for safety. What we saw reminded us never to do what we had done. The place was covered with dung and hoof marks all over the area. Both our water bottles were trampled upon and smashed to a pulp. Thank God our farts did the trick. If not, we would have been buried that day in Seladang dung and laced with our own poop.

Moral of the story......

Always count your blessings. Never question why a disaster that came, just happened to fade away, leaving only a trace of warning for you to be grateful you had left in one piece.

JUNGLE "JAMBAN" GUEST

After our unpleasant ordeal with Mr.Seladang (*Seladang's Dung of Challenge*), I, for one decided never again to venture for a drop job away from base and seriously contemplated to use the manmade *"jamban"* (toilet/latrine) constructed by the boys in my platoon. Not that I was overly enthusiastic about it but what choice did I have, knowing that I may not be that lucky second time round. Imagine what would have happened if *Mr.Seladang* had decided to give chase? All hell would have broken loose; shit to be more precise.

Anyway, coming back to using the jungle loo ala army style, as cadets, we were trained to construct such pit latrines and personally, I was fully aware of the hazardous nature of these jungle loos especially if they were constructed not following the specified and required dimensions, including the hardware used for the said pit. Prior to and during the construction process, measurements needed to be absolutely correct. The depth of the pit, the support beams, including the actual dimensions of the squatting platform "drop" area is extremely narrow; very critical since poor evaluation might just result in the poop missiles landing not on the drop zone way below, but on the back of your ankles or on the foot resting platform.

My greatest fear had always been "what if the platform gave way?" Most of these guys who were actually detailed to construct these latrines never really used it themselves but chose to do their business far away from these latrines for reasons only they knew. Truthfully, they themselves were not too confident of their own work. Can you imagine if the platform did give way? A straight drop, arse first into a pool of fermented, post diarrhoea infected excreta deposited over a two month period by dozens of soldiers based in that location. You need to allow your imagination to take effect to have a feel of the bottom of the pit I am referring to; to get a feel of what I am saying. Even when you gaze at your own mess which you deposit each morning, though you try to decipher and identify what actually makes up that amount of shit; you can only stare for a short time as it is just too sickening to watch however wondrous the "artwork" might look like. My nephew for instance, whenever he did his business, always had the habit of taking a quick look at what he had just created and immediately pukes at what he sees. A totally negative and critical appreciation of his own internal creation.

But in this particular instance, I was quite confident of the overall construction as I had personally supervised the team concerned.

So here I was, perched on the platform underneath of which one could honestly presume to be a replica of what hell would look like, oblivious to it even being there as I kept my gaze and thoughts focused on the scenario around me. And definitely making sure that no uninvited *"seladang"* trotted into my private domain. Talking about gazing at the scenario or scenery; nothing much really since I was inside an enclosed wall of bamboo and "nipah" (palm) leaves serving as a wall with the intention of providing some kind of privacy, as this was a definite pre-requisite when executing this call of nature required by all of us. Not much privacy though, if one were to take into consideration the numerous species of creepy crawlies that were busily moving about their daily tasks but this time quite excited about this latest supply to be painstakingly collected and deposited in their depot. Most of these crawlies were already in and out of the small aperture and they too seemed to give little attention to this big "me" whom to them was a friendly alien providing them with appetizers and nourishment.

As there was no roof above, I could see the blue sky and white clouds of various shapes and sizes; each telling a tale of its own, leaving it to our imagination to decipher its story. Imagine if a downpour were to occur? With no overhead protection and the ground turning wet and soggy especially where one was squatting doing one's business. I, for one, would not for a moment continue doing what I was doing, being afraid the foundations may not hold firm. Not today. Today was a hot sunny day with clear blue skies above. Birds were flying watching below as the world went by and as they flew above me, I could not help wondering if they were aware of what I was doing as a few of them were doing their own depositing. At times I believe they were aiming right at me as some of their air drops fell precariously near to where I was squatting. Talk about precision minus click one, two inches just off target; if it was my head they were aiming at.

What got my attention most were the flies. Yes, flies. How can I leave them out? All kinds. In fact, I believe, every species of the fly family congregated at the "jamban" (latrine) area to touch base, exchange gossips and brag about poop adventures; each with a different shit story to boast about. Among others they included the small *black houseflies, blow flies, hoover flies* and many others, but topping all of them, the infamous *"blue-arsed flies"* usually called the "*lalat jamban*" or latrine flies (*English connotation meaning a **blue** bottle **fly**, which buzzes around rather frantically, like someone who is running around busily doing errands*) that tend to frequent latrines or wherever there is a heap of poop to be found. These flies with their compound eyes practically observing the world go by (or should I say droppings) in a slow and precise fall to the ground, and in a wink of an eye, they are upon the mess. They were everywhere. Zooming around in droves with their very transparent yet multi-coloured wings flapping faster than the naked eye could fathom. They darted so fast in all directions and landing themselves on bird droppings as well as other poop which could have been left by other animals that came into the *"jamban"* area for a look-see and in the process drop their deposits as well. Believe it or not, there were also a few traces of leftover human excreta by soldiers who had a last minute phobia as they were about to take position and squat on the small, intimidating platform but decided to move away to a safer setting and in the process one can imagine what had happened. And this was the most sought after poop the flies would converge upon. For them it was "manna from the heavens". Not my thoughts exactly but just deciphering what goes on in the minds of those flying drones.

As I was observing all that went on around me (whilst taking sips from my water bottle which will come into full use once deposits were completed), I seemed to hear some movement along the far left corner of the makeshift walls of the *"jamban"*. *"Was it a snake or maybe a python?"* I thought as these reptiles loved the *"jambans"* for reasons that totally questioned my reasons for such visits. Imagine a python trying to squeeze shit out of a pool of shit. Or maybe it was a baby wild boar that was wondering around and decided to venture into this enclosure to look for manna of its own; I did not know or even wanted to know. All I knew was that this time round I had come prepared (remember the *Seladang* adventure, or should I say misadventure). I had placed right in front of me my handgun, a Browning .32 pistol; cocked and ready for blasting away any unwelcomed intruder that either intentionally or mistakenly approached me for a face-off. However, I decided to let my weapon rest but kept focused on the area from where the noise of rustling thick tall grass just inside the enclosure came from. My water bottle though, was in my hands just in case it was nothing too threatening whereby I could throw the heavy can towards the intruder to just scare and shoo it away. But it was approaching me slowly and steadily, with the intention of coming closer to me, undeterred or afraid. What was this creature; I started to wonder, a feeling of panic slowly creeping up my spine.

The distance from the make shift bamboo wall to where I was squatting was approximately 15 feet. From what I could observe from the creature's movement, half its body was along the side of the wall and the front of it was a quarter way moving towards me. A baby python I presumed. I could not make out as the boys had not cut the long *"lalang"* (Savannah grass) which they were supposed to as part of their jungle work roster. *"Need to penalise those who were on the list,"* I thought to myself. *"Idiots!"* Reason why I presumed it to be a baby python was because I could visualise the tip of its tail curling up and down on the side of the makeshift bamboo enclosure.

Just for the information of the reader, one may wonder why the square area of the toilet was about 15 feet. Why so large a space to accommodate just one shit hole or latrine to be more precise? Wrong! Not one, but three latrines were actually constructed inside this enclosure; in a parallel row and separated by "camouflage ponchos". Unless you were close buddies and needed some privacy together to discuss intimate details concerning some operational issues (I never did), no one ever attempted (not that I can vouch for) doing their business with another on the other side of the poncho. So basically, the toilet area was quite large and so too the "whatever" that was creeping towards me.

Back to the present. Too close for comfort; baby python or not, from my water bottle, I splashed some water to where I presumed the head was and lo behold, it raised its head either because it was agitated, shocked or bewildered. What I saw scared the shit out of me (or whatever there was left). It was the head of a massive black *"biawak"* or monitor lizard; and this guy was huge!. From my immediate estimation, clearly a six footer and its head was as big as a full grown Alsatian's. And it was quite agitated from the saliva it was salivating. Knowing they were carnivorous, I was expecting the worst if I did not do anything to stop it from a full frontal charge. The reason I was so sure of its intentions was because this was the very same *"biawak"* that used to sit and observe us when we went for our baths or to collect water in the nearby river. It used to be perched on a very high boulder, most times with some meat in its mouth; gnawing away with vigorous ferocity giving not a damn in the world whether we existed or not. It was definitely not afraid of us and so too during this instance. I saw this whole scenario in my thoughts, as would a fly with its immaculate compound eyes; all in slow motion.

My right hand went to my handgun but refrained from shooting knowing at the back of my mind what a laughing stock I would be once back in camp. 'The officer who shot a *"biawak"* that invaded his privacy in the privy.' But instead, I threw my water bottle with all my strength at the "predator" (and that's exactly what it was!). Not an easy task. Try throwing a bottle of water with your left hand while squatting in a precarious position on a makeshift latrine. In a whisk, it clambered on all fours, practically floating towards the next cubicle and I heard a loud *"sloush"*. The bugger must have dived headon into the latrine cavity next to where I was squatting and landed itself inside the cess pool of fermented shit. The next moment, I heard a hissing sound below, between my legs, and the *predator's* head pops out. In a bolt, I do a quick leap frog, grabbing my pants and holding on to it and practically skipped out of the *"jamban's"* enclosure and straight to the river a short distance away. A quick look back to see if I was being followed, and straight into the water to clear the mess. Poop was already dropping from my arse and thighs. I would have to collect my water bottle later.

"Tuan mandi atau berak? " (Sir, you had a bath or went to shit?), quipped my bat-man with a knowing look in his eyes. I was totally drenched but still in one piece. I could not help wondering why some of my boys gave me a knowing, sympathetic glance as I walked past them. Then it hit me; the human excreta that was left on the ground

near the latrines. They too had a similar tale to share, I guess. I was not in this *"biawak"* pit alone.

Moral of the story......?

They say the jungle is neutral. It is only neutral for that which belongs there. As outsiders, we are actually trespassing into their domain. A domain that does not belong to us. Likewise, when we go into another's, where we are not really invited or welcomed, always watch our entire movement and the place we are in; lest we step on toes or the unnatural, ultimately landing ourselves in deep shit.

SON'S POP-UP ORDEAL

He had taken a quiet stroll along Chow Kit Road one warm afternoon hoping to get a juice drink from the 7/11 store just around the corner. Walking along the pavement, oblivious to the surroundings, he suddenly felt as if he was sucked down a deep tunnel into Hell. He felt a tremendous jerk of his left knee, and without any chance of pulling back, he fell hard and fast on his already twisted knee, which now was facing the full onslaught of his 90 kg body weight. The sheer shock and pain knocked him off for a few seconds. When he opened his eyes, he was wailing as he could feel the pain shoot right through his brains; but best of all, he could not stand upright and had to be assisted by some passersby who hailed a cab and sent him off to the hospital. He was diagnosed with having a torn tendon which required surgery, scheduled to be conducted a week from the date of this mishap. He was admitted pending the scheduled date fixed.

Being in the orthopaedic surgical ward was quite okay. The toilets were near and with the aid of crutches he could make it to the cubicles. But each time he visited the cubicles, he used to wonder how, once after surgery, could he use the toilet as each cubicle was quite a small square. Not able to stretch the leg if it was in a POP (Plaster of Paris caste). The thought of that used to keep him awake most of the nights of how he was going to cross that hurdle. Definitely he would have to stay in the hospital for at least 3 to 4 days before being discharged. One of his strategies was to make sure that whatever he ate for the day was quickly "disposed" off so that he could withstand not going to the toilet once he was operated on. And no way was he going to use the pan to do his business in bed.

Surgeries were usually conducted in the early mornings; so he thought. By noon if he was not forewarned or made ready for surgery, he took it that it would be the next morning. So during lunch, he had his full meal with a lot of spicy side snacks included. And of course, the usual afternoon tea break savouries like curry puffs and the likes, were on the menu as well. Usually, if he were to be operated the next morning, or if at all he may come under the scheduled list, the attendant would give him an enema to relieve his bowels. So each late evening, he was extremely careful not to indulge in any food other than mild liquids especially after he had discharged remnants of what he had eaten for the day. No worries for the following day surgery and with an empty stomach, he was very sure that he could withstand any urge to go to the loo after surgery.

So that fateful evening, lying on his bed, busily munching and gulping hot chicken curry puffs, *vadai* (Indian savoury doughnut) and hot *teh tarik* (frothy tea), he noticed the hospital attendant coming through the ward entrance with a tray of shaving items. He was wondering who the poor fellow who was going to be dissected that night. *"Might be an emergency case,"* he concluded. And as his mouth kept munching and chewing and masticating, his eyes slowly widened and the patient in front of him could have sworn that he saw pieces of what was being masticated suddenly pop out of his mouth as the attendant walked to the side of his bed.

The surgery went well. The leg was in a cast and other than being able to hop around with a pair of crutches, going to the loo was out of the question for the next four days following the surgery. No way could he possibly get himself seated on the toilet seat without his cast leg jutting out of the cubicle. This was totally out of the question..

"Nah Encik. You bolih guna ini bila mahu buang air besar." (Here Sir, you can use this when you want to do the big one). Saying that, the *"amah"* (ward maid) placed the pan, covered with a sheet on the bed and walked off as if it was no big deal; for her, at least. For the next four days, the bedpan "waited" patiently under the bed, totally untouched. Even in the middle of the night when all hell was about to break loose for the eruption of a second "Krakatua", he just refused to allow the unthinkable to

materialise. Every night, he cursed himself all the time for his lack of self-control where eating was concerned. Every night he makes the same promise for not wanting to overindulge in food; breakfast, lunch and dinner, including the in-between snacks that bloat up within his tummy moving precariously closer and closer to the inevitable canal of release. But it was only through sheer discipline and the nightmarish thought of using a bed pan that gave him the courage to withstand each moment when the sudden urge to discharge erupted. Oh, what a Man!

Finally, after four days of sphincter control, on a bright Saturday morning, his discharge papers were prepared and his family; wife, son (who knew not what was in store for him) and daughter wheeled him to the waiting car for the short drive home.

"*Short drive? Short drive?*" was all he could say when his wife told him that it being a short drive home she wanted to stop over at the *nasi campur* (mixed rice) stall to buy lunch. "*Either you drive straight home or five days of molten lava will be strewn all over the back seat of your Persona (Malaysian car model). And make it quick! I do not know how much longer I can hold it.*" As these frantic words calling for haste were uttered, all heard a shirking cry from his daughter... "*Aiyoo Papa, what is that smell?*"

The gates were flung open by the maid who had been notified of the "emergency" (thank God for handphones) as his wife came to a screeching halt in front of the house when she slammed down on the brakes. He was already beginning to sweat profusely as he scrambled out of the car with his son holding his crutches ceremoniously in front of him which he grabbed and hopped in lightning bolt fashion heading towards the front door. His maid came to greet him with a broad smile… *"hello tuan. Selamat kembali."* (Hello Sir. Welcome back). His response? *"Ya. Ya. Lalu cepat."* (Yes. Yes. Move it). She knew her boss all too well. Her broad smile knowingly turned to a gleeful laughter.

TALES OF THE LOO

"Dai, go bring that black plastic bag...quick. And some rubber bands or raffia string," he instructed his son as he went to the downstairs toilet only to realise that he could not use since his injured leg currently in a cast (POP – Plaster of Paris), would not allow him to perch comfortably on the "throne" as the wall was too close and he could not bend his knee.

Out of the downstairs bathroom and practically hopping up the stairs with his son following closely behind fully equipped with plastic bags and rubber bands. His son not knowing exactly what they were for.

Into the second toilet (a bit more sensibly constructed with enough space), he hopped and trotted and slammed down the seat, *sarong* already down somewhere along the stairs while telling his son to wrap his POP with plastic to avoid getting his injured leg wet. *"Quick Da, put the plastic. Quickly, it is coming. Tak bolih, Da."* (Cannot, Da)

"Wait la Papa, wait. Aiyooamma the smell! How to put the plastic....."

VROOOM PRAT PROP...... "Aiyooooo, Ammaaaa!" Papa exclaims.

A sigh of extreme relief and sudden emptiness as he felt a vacuum deep down his bowels. What else to expect when the remains of five days had been finally discharged.

"Thanks Da. Can you now remove the plastic? Son, son....... Dai...where are you?'

Moral of the Story......

Everyone has a limit. There is only so much anyone can take; immaterial who they are to you. Including sons and daughters.

WIND BREAK-A-LOO - THE MEDAN DIP

A Decisive Morning

The whole house was abuzz with excitement. Grandpa and the two elder cousins were in their last minute packing for their first plane ride out of the country to Medan. *"Lake Toba, here we come!"* exclaimed Mark as he helped Nisha (his cousin) with her bags. Both were in their teens and all this was a new adventure for them. New country to explore, different culture, food and people. More importantly, their first plane ride and with all that excitement around them, both were feeling a wee bit nervous. Although they kept it to themselves, a knot was slowly forming in their tummies. Both went to bed early as they had an early flight to catch the next morning.

The morning started off well. All were up by 4.30 am; each engaged in their respective morning SOP (Standard Operating Procedure) .... addressing the call of nature, brushing their teeth, followed by hot showers. The flight from the Subang Aerodrome was scheduled for 0800 hours. As stipulated, check-in was one hour earlier. Mark's father was already having his bath while the kids were having their breakfast. Nisha stuck to her cereals as she still felt the nervous knot of excitement in her tummy. Mark on the other hand, felt wonderful and dug his teeth into a turkey ham sandwich, topped with fried egg, cheese and mayonnaise.

"Hey! Go slow on the food. Do not stuff yourself too much. Anyway, Grandpa has included inflight food for you guys," his mum reminded him. But there was no stopping Mark as he finished off his breakfast and was eyeing the Coco Crunch which Nisha had in her bowl. The nervous knot in his stomach had long since unwound itself and he was looking forward to getting out of the house, into the car and to the airport. This was one trip he was not going to be late for.

As Mark's father was washing the soap off his face and body, all of a sudden, there was a wailing sound from the corridor as if someone had just died.

"Oh my God! Where did you put my passport? It is not with me. Did you not pack it together with my clothes?" exclaimed Mark's Grandfather. Mark's father continued to shower with a smile on his face (how mean could one get? Affording a smile during a time of crisis?), as he heard his father-in-law blame the wife for not packing the passport.

"Your passport, you pack la. Why blame me?" exclaimed Grandma angrily.

"Aiyooo, how can this happen now? What am I to do? Already paid for and how are the children going to go?" wailed Grandpa over and over again until Mark's mum had to calm him down. Mark's father, although already completed his bath, had his ears peeled to the door to hear what was going on outside. He heard his wife tell his father-in-law that they will need to call the trip organisers and seek their advice.

"Papa, can you come out from the bathroom? We have a major problem," Mark knocked on the bathroom door, hoping that his father would have a solution.

"Ya, I overheard," quipped Mark's father as he came out of the bath. *"No worries,"* he said and his solution executed another disgusting wail from Grandpa. *"Both the kids can go on their own la. Big enough and since it is a church outing, with the church members to look out for them."*

"Then what about me? This is supposed to be a pilgrimage to the holy 'Vellangganni' church in Medan and I cannot go? Can you not do something? Why la Honey, (Grandpa's affectionate name for Grandma*) you could not check before we left home?"* Grandpa continued, totally dejected and frustrated. All this while, Mark's mum was on the phone with the organisers and the contact person; a personal friend.

Both Mark and Nisha looked totally devastated. *"Is this trip not going to materialise?"* The same thought went through their minds as well. Suddenly Mark's stomach started to churn as it usually happens when a catastrophe was about to happen. This was a major unimaginable tsunami in the making. All the same, he controlled his bowels as he wanted to know the outcome of this ordeal, and wished Grandpa would just stop this wailing; making everyone feel miserable.

"Okay. Done." Mark's mother exclaimed with an air of authority having just got off the line with the organiser. *"Papa, we need to go to Kluang (Grandpa's hometown about 270 km away) to collect your passport. Apparently, you can catch the later flight in the evening and meet up with the rest in Medan tonight. Need to reschedule the ticket itinerary. Peter (the tour organiser) will get this done. Not to worry."* Mum was at her element - mother, daughter, teacher, all rolled into one. Mark's father was quiet and knew he had to drive to Kluang with his father-in-law to get the passport.

"But what about the kids?" Grandpa continued. *"Are they also flying off in the evening?"* *"No,"* mum explained. *"They go off in the morning as planned and will wait for you in Medan. Both are old enough and I am quite confident of Mark watching over Nisha. Moreover, it is a church group and most know Mark."*

Mark and Nisha were practically jumping with joy although a little apprehensive, as this was the first time they were both travelling without parental presence. Nervous, scared, excited were all adverse feelings bundled into one major ecstasy. Mark's tummy woes slowly crept into a deep end of his tummy and just grumbled not being allowed to be released before the trip. A feeling of uneasiness was already brewing within the knot it had formed into; just waiting to be discharged. But Mark was too excited to notice the rumbling within and got ready for the long awaited trip.

Mark's mum would accompany her husband and father (Grandpa) to Kluang, but only after seeing Mark and Nisha off at the Subang Aerodrome. At the terminal, having met with Peter, who was joking about the passport Grandpa left behind and practically making him (Grandpa) feel extremely uneasy and embarrassed. Last minute instructions were given by both Mum and Papa; including of course the hugs and kisses. *"See you later, Grandpa. Don't get lost."* Nisha joked as she and Mark with the rest of the tour group exited towards the terminal gate. They will get to see Grandpa later that evening.

The Flight - Premonition

Once in their respective seats, both Mark and Nisha started to laugh and joke about the early morning pre-adventure episode concerning Grandpa's passport, including the ruckus and commotion he had raised. *"Poor Papa. Alone with Mummy and Grandpa all the way to Kluang and* back. *A real long and tedious journey. Hope no breakdown along the way, knowing the Wira* (car model) *has its own hiccups,"* were Mark's thoughts as he waited to be served the morning's inflight meal. Ever hungry as usual, although having had a good solid breakfast that morning itself. Looking out of the window, Mark knew that with all the rattling and shakiness, they were on a Fokker. The wing span was quite short and the propellers could be visibly seen from where he was seated. All this rumbling and massage-like movements created by what most Fokkers were known for, slowly but surely awakened *'Mr. Knot'* that was cosily snuggled up within his already hungry tummy, having not been discharged the morning before the trip. Going to the toilet did not do any good that morning because of the excitement and all that other commotions that had ensured.

The inflight morning menu consisted of *'Nasi lemak'* (coconut rice) with *'belacan kangkong'* (water spinach cooked in chilly fish paste) and *'sambal ikan bilis'* (anchovies) topped with a fried *'bull's eye'*; really spicy and hot. Mark took his time devouring and savouring the spiciness and aromatic flavour that emancipated from the food. Once the meal was over having added an extra deposit into his tummy, creating a further avalanche of slime gathering within his bowels. The Fokker's vibrating flight mode did not help in any way. The knot was slowly beginning to unwind itself very slowly as would a python uncoiling itself, sensing a prey within its reach. In this instance, the prey was not food to be squeezed and swallowed whole, but more so to be excreted.

The flight to Medan was an hour plus. Mark, after the heavy yet hearty inflight spicy *nasi lemak,* began to feel uneasy. His tummy began to grumble angrily, complaining for having been used as an unlimited deposit bank. A major discharge was on the card. The urge to break wind was making him feel uneasy but he knew that if he did so all hell would definitely break loose. They were seated just three rows away from the cockpit and the toilet was situated way at the back. This being the first time on a plane, Mark was a little shy to walk up to the toilet, knowing fully well all who were sitting from where he was would instantly know that he was going to discharge his spicy loot. So Mark just decided to control himself. Anyway, there was just another twenty odd minutes before landing. *"I should be able to hold on until we land,"* he thought. He was practically twirling in his seat, shifting his buttocks and forcing himself to painfully clamp shut his sphincter cavity lest he discharges, losing control of his physical ability not to do so.

Without a warning, there was a slight air turbulence which made the Fokker suddenly drop and rattle uncontrollably making Mark lose control of his ability to hold his fart, and break wind he did. Not in a loud way but more of a slow and long *'pweeeeet..... prut-prut'*; thankfully unheard by anyone due to the rattling sound of the Fokker. The plane was back on course. But the damage had already been done.

"What's that smell?" Nisha whispered into Mark's ear. He was already sweating profusely and Nisha wondered if he was going throw up or something. *"Hey, are you okay?"* she asked. Mark only nodded in the affirmative, smiling like a hyena about to explode with shit. Again Nisha raised the question ... *"What is that smell?!. Like rotten eggs."* Having learnt during their Science class that within the confines of a pressurised compartment, any smell emitted would remain intact and eventually find its way into open cavities such as the nostrils. The smell was slowly meandering its way to the rear of the plane where close to thirty odd passengers were waiting to be 'suffocated' to glory.

"Ooi ... Celaka! Siapa kuntut? Betul-betul bau punya bau!" yelled one 'victim' from the rear. (Ooi ... Idiot! Who farted? So smelly!)

"Mahu berak pegi tandas la. Bukan lepas saja. Bodoh!" continued another. (Want to shit go to the toilet la. Don't just let go like that. Stupid!)

"Who farted?" Nisha enquired from Mark. *"You ah?"*

"No la. Not me. Someone from the back I think," Mark denied, hiding his embarrassment, by telling a white lie to Nisha. Just then, the intercom sounded and the Captain informed everyone that the plane would be landing shortly, instructing all to fasten their seat belts. Saved by the bell! The 'python' calmed itself and went back to sleep for the

next wave to erupt. Mark was his usual self again and forgot about the very short ordeal a moment ago.

The Fokker landed without a hitch; save for one or two bumps, otherwise a smooth landing altogether. As it eased its way on the tarmac, manoeuvring slowly towards the main terminal entrance, most of the passengers were already clambering to take their hand luggage, queuing patiently for the door to open. Once the door was opened the passengers exited, each taking in a gulp of fresh air, exultant to escape from the still obnoxious smell lingering within the cabin.

"Phew …. I thought we would never get out of that. Terrible smell la, Mark. I wonder who was so inconsiderate?" Nisha complained to her cousin as they walked down the steps from the plane to the hard tarmac. Mark kept absolutely silent. On his mind, *"do I head towards the toilet or can it wait?"* were his only thoughts. But once into the terminal while waiting for their luggage to arrive, the excitement once again erased Mark of his thoughts of going to the loo for a quick 'let go'. He should have; but he didn't. Major regrets to follow. The bus was already waiting for the tour group outside the terminal for the long and treacherous journey up to Lake Toba. Once they had collected their luggage (including Grandpa's, who would be landing on a later flight to meet them the next morning, as he would have to stay over one night in Medan), they got onto the bus for their long awaited journey.

Mark's Attire

I should at this juncture, give the reader a quick description of what Mark actually wore for this trip. For a long flight and bus journey, such as the one about to be embarked on, anyone for that matter, would dress quite casually with the sole purpose of being as comfortable as possible. Nothing too elaborate or fancy. Especially dressing up as if one were going on an African jungle safari. That's exactly how Mark was geared up. A quick description of his attire should give you an impression of the difficulty he was about to encounter during the 'pit stop' along the journey.

> ➢ Let's start with his footwear. Standard army boots with shoe laces tightly wound into each lace hole to the maximum.

> ➢ Wrangler jeans; tight fitting 'drain pipe' version.

> ➢ The jeans were already bulging at the waist but it was further tightened by a leather belt with a huge swirling Manchester United metal buckle.

> ➢ British army jacket over a chequered shirt tucked into an already tight jeans.

> ➢ Back pack.

➢ A cowboy hat which he had bought from one of his trips to *Jonker Street* in Melaka.

➢ And to top it all, sun glasses.

You need to imagine how ridiculous he looked but that was Mark, the dresser. The journey to Lake Toba began on a bus that had no air conditioning, quite packed and practically rattled all the way as it wound its way along the treacherous mountain road towards its destination.

The rattling was worse when compared to the Fokker. The Fokker was moving through air. This bus was moving on hard road with pot holes every inch of the way. The continuous shakiness and unsettling nature of the drive made Mark uncomfortably uneasy especially with his extremely ridiculous attire that inadvertently awakened the sleeping, knotted 'python' coiled deep within him. The rumbling began once again earnestly. The regret of not having visited the loo at the terminal made Mark sweat profusely once again. At least this time if he were to break wind, the stench would not linger nor permeate into open nostrils as the bus windows were all down to allow air to cool the passengers.

Pit Stop Blues

Mark kept on shifting uneasily in his seat much to the irritation of Nisha who was seated next to him. She was already feeling extremely nervous looking out of the window and seeing the steep drop from where the bus was meandering along the road towards its destination. And each time Mark shifted his buttocks, it further aggravated the 'python' that was already free of its coiled knot and awaiting a final discharge, with or without Mark making a decision whether to hold until journey's end.

After almost one-half hours on the journey, with Mark practically feeling ooze slightly wetting his underwear and knowing that at any time he would not be able to hold on to this magnificent dash of hot mutant lava, which the 'python' had suddenly evolved into.

Suddenly, the bus turned into an open area by the side of the road and stopped. Mark could see a few make shift wooden and zinc shops where food was being sold. His eyes kept darting to see if there was any latrine nearby or worse comes to worst, some jungle cover where he could discharge what was already brewing into Mount Krakatoa at its peak.

Then he saw it. So too a dozen others who just like Mark wanted to use the makeshift latrine as well. He was up from his seat in a jiffy but because of his very heavy gear, found some difficulty clambering out of the bus where ahead of him there were two other passengers, not including another three, already waiting in line at the entrance to the **'Bilek Ayer Pubik'** (Public Lavatory). While waiting for his turn, Mark kept on cursing himself for having dressed so ridiculously and wondering how he was going to strip once inside. This was because from what he saw, the so-called latrine had only standing room dimensions. What more if one attempted to squat with all that gear he was decked under. He was already straining to clamp shut his sphincter cavity but knew he could not last much longer. Other than cold sweat, he was also beginning to shiver, straining to keep the contents within without bursting out of his interns.

The Open Air Discharge Pit – WATCH OUT FOR THAT DROP!!!

When Mark slowly eased his way into the latrine enclosure (any quick movement and he would have had to let go there itself), he noticed that there was a low wall surrounding the latrine area. So low that any passenger from the bus could have had a good view of those entering the toilet and into the cubicle to relieve themselves. Too open and without any privacy where he could comfortably remove his shoes and pants before going in. Moreover, just next to the latrine was the urinal pots and there were one or two guys already easing themselves. Mark could see right over the low wall that was extending from either side of the cubicle, and what he saw was just open air space and nothingness. Just a sheer drop to nowhere.

As the cubicle was in use, Mark waited patiently outside twirling his belt buckle and he intelligently decided to untie his bootlaces but was not quick enough as the door of the cubicle opened and it was ready for Mark to make his entrance to execute discharge. He had to go in double quick because there were one or two others also waiting to use the latrine. Imagine … only one latrine.

When he thought that there was going to be no tomorrow, the door opens and out comes the one using the latrine earlier.

"Halo, jaga-jaga dalam nanti. Tada jaga, jatuh lo." (Hello, be careful once inside. Not careful, you may fall) his parting words to Mark before leaving the enclosure.

Mark opened the door and lo! what he saw sent shivers up his spine. At once, he felt a gush of strong cold wind blow from the latrine directly into his face and the wind was coming from particularly nowhere but from the open space at the back of the toilet. Other than a very low wall of about two feet, there was only emptiness and white skies with a sheer drop just after the wall. The cubicle was extremely narrow. One enters, stands and squats; and that's that. A small pipe by the side allowed minimal hand movement to wash after the discharge was complete.

For a split second, due to the shock of seeking such a cubicle, the 'python' recoiled, waiting with a vengeance to explode. During this very short span of time, Mark did a yoga drill that would have put any yoga master to shame.

First, he quickly squatted, pants intact to untie his bootlaces. He then stood up (knees already aching) and with the aid of one leg after the other, removed his boots with great difficulty and stood on them on either side of the foot rest. Next, he unbuckled his belt and removed his pants which were getting stuck at his knees and ankles because they were tight fitting. He managed to remove and wrap his drainpipes around his neck with the waistend on his head above his cowboy hat like a turban. His underwear was stripped and lowered down around his thighs. His sunglasses, due to the movement of his pants drooped from his eyes and came just below his nose. Then he squatted; but not a second too soon because the moment he squatted and eased his sphincter cavities, the muscles of his buttocks and rear took control. There was no controlling the hot gush of putrid smelling liquid waste that just shot out, and continued to flow from within him, and directly straight into the bottomless pit of the latrine he was perched upon. He was sweating but his back felt extremely cold due to the open rear of the cubicle. If for any reason he had accidentally fallen backwards, the chances of recovering Mark would have been impossible because of the sheer drop to the bottom of the ravine...... Mark, shit and all!

Once he had finished, he slowly retracted his earlier yoga moves and dressed himself up, but not before excruciatingly turning to turn on the tap and wash his rear. He left the cubicle with a sigh of relief. His Medan ordeal over and a lesson to be learnt; watch your food intake before any long journey and do not overly dress, lest you end up in a ravine just for answering the call of Nature.

Moral of the story......

Long journeys are usually very unpredictable, may it be a holiday trip or on business. What to expect along the journey, we will never be able to predict. Dress adequately and make sure you do not indulge in consuming too much food and drinks before taking off lest you end up performing yoga poses in unmentionable places.

CLING CLANG - FIRE IN THE HOLE

"So David, looks like you have the whole hostel to yourself for the next few days until the others come back after the semester break," Saint Phil's hostel warden, Candy kidded with David as he escorted him up the steps to his dormitory. "I think only two other rooms are occupied but they are on the other wing. Reserved for seniors. Anyway, you will meet up with them soon. One of them is Lim, also from Malaysia, and the other, Iqbal, from Mauritius," continued Candy as he opened the door for David to show his room where he would be staying for the duration of his 2 year pre-university studies in Mysore, Karnataka State, India.

Earlier that morning, David's brother Daniel had taken an "auto" ride from the hotel where they had been staying the night before. David, having just landed two days earlier in Chennai, where his brother had picked him up from the airport and together took a train ride up to Mysore where Daniel had enrolled his brother into Saint Phil's College. After a solid breakfast of "Masala Dosai" (vegetarian stuffed fermented rice pancake) gulped down with Mysore Bru coffee, and now sitting in the warden's office, David felt a little down and nervous as this was his first trip away from home. Besides, Daniel would be leaving that afternoon back to Mangalore where he was currently doing his final month of housemanship. Daniel was expected to fly back to Malaysia as a full-fledged MBBS graduate within the next two months, and Mangalore was a full two day journey from Mysore, and David suddenly felt very much alone and isolated.

David deposited his bag in the room which was situated at the far end just next to the toilets on the third floor. He was in the second building of the four massive hostel blocks. Candy invited David and his brother for lunch at a nearby restaurant across the road about two kilometres from the hostel blocks. Though it was basic Indian food, David felt it was a bit too spicy and the water quite difficult to swallow. Later he was to learn that water in Mysore was actually pure mineral water from the well and thus the heaviness in texture.

Once lunch was over, Daniel got on the bus that stopped just in front of the restaurant, gave David a strong handshake and bid farewell. Candy accompanied David back to his dormitory and told him that dinner would not be provided for the time being in the hostel canteen as it was still closed. However, he could later pack some food in the evening from the restaurant where they had had their lunch. With that, Candy went back to his office and David miserably went to his room on the third floor. It was already touching three in the afternoon and since his tummy was feeling very uncomfortable, David decided to lie down for a while.

As he lay down on his bed which was covered with an extremely thin mattress and a very hard pillow under his head, David studied his room that was white washed with dark green borders. There was a window which allowed a good deal of light into the room. There was another bed next to his on the opposite side of the wall. There were two tables, two chairs and two extremely narrow built-in cabinets. There were also some candles and a matchbox on the table. Very Spartan, unlike his room back home; David was suddenly feeling extremely homesick. The uneasiness in his stomach was not making it easier either. "Maybe I will skip dinner," thought David as he was feeling very uncomfortable. The warmth of the late afternoon sun made him drowsy and soon he was in deep slumber; tired, lonely and miserable. To top it all, an aching tummy.

"Tweeeet, tweeeet, clang, clang".

"Tweeeet, tweeeet, clang, clang"

"Tweeeet, tweeeet, clang, clang".

The sound was very distant but extremely penetrating especially in the chill of the night, and it was coming from outside the main dorm area moving ghostly towards the hostel block where David was staying.

The sound though quite a distance away, aroused David from his deep slumber. The distant sound had still not registered in his mind but the darkness made him sit up in bed as he turned to look at the window. The sun's bright rays were now replaced with pitch darkness and looking at his illuminated watch, the time showed 11.45 pm.

"Wow!" exclaimed David. "I must have slept off. So late .... and where the hell is the switch for the lights?" were David's thoughts as he clambered out of his bed looking for the switch next to the door.

Click, click. Nothing. The lights were not functioning. David kept on switching the lights on and off, but to no avail. Apparently, there seemed to be some kind of power failure. And then he remembered seeing the candles and matchbox on the table. His eyes were more or less accustomed to the darkness and he could visualise the candles and matchbox that was left on the table. From this, he put two and two together and told himself to get used to lightless nights in the future. As he slowly clawed his way towards the table to take the candle, he nearly did a flip when all of a sudden he heard in the near distance a penetratingly eerie sound .... *"Tweeeeet, tweeeet, clang, clang."* Then after a short while again ... *"tweeeeeet, tweeeeet, clang, clang"* followed by an eerie silence. He stopped in his tracks and waited for it to sound again. Nothing.

"Maybe it is only my imagination," he thought.

He took the matchbox, removed a match stick and lit a candle. The sudden glow sent a chill up his spine since the sudden shadowy light created strange haunting images on the wall. It was really creepy to look at, more so when all he could see outside the window was the next white hostel block with darkened closed windows. And only then did he realise that he had a sudden urge to take a leak. "Would the corridor lights be on or were they also not working like the one in his room?" he thought to himself. Slowly, he removed the latch of his door and opened the door to the corridor. Pitch darkness. As he strained to look towards the lavatories that were just a few feet away, he suddenly heard the eerie clanging sound again...... *"Clang, Clang, tweeeet, tweeeet."* This time the sound came from below where he was standing, the ground floor dorm. Without a moment's hesitation, David quickly shut the door, fastened the latch and waited. In his haste, the candle light had extinguished. He suddenly felt cold and his stomach muscles started to cramp with fear. "What was that sound?" he kept asking himself. From his window he could see that none of the rooms opposite his block was occupied. If one was lighted, he could have screamed for help or something. But all he could do was sweat profusely even though it was getting quite cold and his stomach was beginning to churn. He felt extremely cold and wet, and angrily realised that he had wet his pants. "God, this cannot be happening!" he thought and he started to silently curse his brother for having left him here all on his own. His first visit to a foreign country and this had to happen.

"Tweeeeet, tweeeet, clang, clang" and it was now on the second floor moving up the stairway. David was certain of that. Soon "it" or whatever it was, would come his way looking for a victim to devour or strangle; he was not sure. He was getting shit scared and the urge to relieve himself, the fear made his tummy rumble and groan and he knew for a fact that he might just let go there itself. He looked at his watch. It was 30 minutes past the bewitching hour. A cold uncanny wind was blowing through the window into the room and once again the sound of *"clang, clang"* was approaching. He was now shuddering with fright and apprehension of meeting death in the eye.

As the wind howled outside, the sound of death came closer and closer; climbing up the final stairs and onto the third floor where David's dorm was located. Since he did not dare light the candle, David was wondering where he could hide in case the demon walked into the room, sickle in hand. The sound grew intensively louder and the absolute fear in him made his bowels turn upside down, reflecting the fear within himself. He was just seventeen years old and never before had he encountered anything so fearful such as what he was experiencing at that moment.

Then "it" was at his door. *"Tweeeeet! Tweeeeet! CLANG! CLANG!"* "It" was banging on the door. David jumped onto the bed clutching his pillow against his chest as protection (inwardly knowing how stupid he was in believing that a cotton pillow would be of any help).

The banging and the clanging went on forever, and though he tried screaming, the scream was stuck in his throat unable to be released..... "Aiyoooo Amma, Amma," he screamed silently. However much he tried to scream and call for help, he just could not release the sound from within him but he did however release what was within, but through the rear. All shit came out loose in a mutant liquid form, messing him including the thin mattress he was now on. He was still clinging to his pillow for dear life.

He heard someone from the other side of the door call out... "hello baiya (brother). Teek Hae?" (Are you ok?). This was repeated a couple of times with knocks on the door. David was just too scared to utter a word and just sat on the bed shivering for dear life. A sharp piercing pain was felt in his rear as one would feel when diluted shit exits without control. At that moment he was least concerned about what he was unconsciously releasing into the open, as his thoughts were focused on the "thing" calling him on the other side of the door.

Suddenly there was total silence. It was just for a short while, when he heard some rattling sound like chains being released and dropped on the ground, *"Claaaang, clang, clang, clang"*. Silence again. Silence for an eternity. Nothing was heard from the other side of the door. David did not dare move because it could be a trick enticing him to open the door. And once open, for "it" to savagely pounce and devour him as would a wild animal attacking its victim; body, soul, shit and all.

After almost an eternity he heard once again, *"tweeeeet, tweeeeet, clang, clang"*. This time the sound was moving away from where his room was. Each time he heard the clanking and sound of the piercing whistle, it went further and further away from the block. It was gone. Not in David's mind though, as he kept hearing it in his head and expected "it" to suddenly reappear in front of his door when he least expected or let his guard down. He decided he was not going to budge from where he was until he could see daylight.

He was in this position for a long, long time. Although he was feeling cramps all over, he still did not dare get off the bed. The putrid smell of liquefied excreta that was now totally "embracing" him, as well as the mattress, reached his nostrils and he felt like puking. He also felt a bit dizzy. He looked at his watch. It was 5.40 am. "My God!" he exclaimed to himself. As if in response, he could feel and see the breaking of day with rays of sunlight slowly shooting into his room. The world was awakening and he felt it was time for him to get up from where he was seated. Slowly he tried to raise himself from the bed because it was a truly uncomfortable effort to try and get up from one's own shit plastered all over oneself as well as on the bed. He had no choice and got off the bed carefully. The liquid excreted by him was clinging onto him and he could feel some of the slime oozing down his legs as well. It was now quite bright. He looked around, surveying on the next logical cause of action. He had to clean himself up as well as get rid of the now totally soiled mattress that was steaming with such a putrefied and pungent smell, that it was enveloping the whole room with a stench.

The first thing he did was to strip himself naked. He placed his soiled clothes on the thin mattress, which he rolled up easily. He opened his suitcase which had been left unopened, took out his towel and liquid bath soap. He did not wrap his towel around himself because of the plastered shit all over his lower body, including his groin. He placed the towel and liquid soap on the table. He slowly opened the door, looking to the left and right. The whole floor was totally empty. He then went back to the bed, took the rolled up mattress and at the same time took the matchbox that was on the table. He quickly tip-toed out of his room and headed towards the latrines just a few rooms away.

He went to the last latrine, opening the door slowly. It was quite dark in the cubicle but it was clean as it had not been used for the last month due to the semester break. He inserted the soiled mattress with his clothes into the toilet bowl. He lit a match and set fire to the cotton mattress and in an instant it caught fire and started to burn, engulfing in flames and smoke that quickly filled the whole latrine, suffocating David. Burning shit smells very peculiar but there was now a **fire in the hole** which was his intention. He watched as the whole mattress burnt to a cinder. There was no water in the bowl because the latrine works on a pour flush system. Since it had not used for such a long time, the bowl was completely dry. His task completed. All evidence burnt and except for the funny smell of burnt shit and smoke, there was nothing to show or tell of his ordeal the night before.

He went back to his room to collect his towel and soap and walked naked to the bathroom opposite the latrines. He took the pail that was provided. He then went to the bathroom, collected water and poured into the toilet bowl where only "shit ash" was still present but only for a moment. Water from the bucket did the trick. He went back to the bathroom and had a shower like one he had never had before; washing and cleansing himself thoroughly.

After a good bath, he was back in his room and changed into his clothes. There was a knock on the door....

"David, your warden here." David opened the door and greeted his warden.

"What is that funny smell?" Candy asked, not to David in particular but just an inquisitive question. "Come, let me take you for breakfast," he continued. "Seems a bit smoky here. Must be the gardener clearing up and burning the leaves downstairs outside," he answered his own question.

David came out of his room and locked the door. As he and his hostel warden were walking along the corridor, Candy placed his hand on David's shoulder and said, "I forgot to tell you. We have a night watchman who does his rounds and you may have heard him last night blowing his whistle and rattling his old bell. I hope he did not scare or disturb your sleep."

"Not at all, Sir," David replied, but in his mind he told himself.... "Now you tell me, you idiot."

Moral of the story......?

Always, always, always ask questions especially if you are new to a place. It's not the other party who is an idiot, but you, for not being inquisitive. Did curiosity kill the cat? Not that I know of but you become better informed about your surroundings and what to expect. Always ask the better question to stay safe and clean.

BREAKNECK DISCHARGE

He had driven at breakneck speed; his eyes and mind focused on the road ahead of him. He knew that this was a test like none other he had experienced. But that is what he had thought; for he had in the past, like so many before him, and yet to come, who had encountered this unheralded phenomenon; a tsunami from within. This test of endurance and mind over matter; not all have succeeded in beating the speed of the outward splurge that very often gives the "splurgee" ample warnings to stop, consider the options (and the distance), the numerous R&R (Rest and Recreation) stops that he had passed by. But no, the "splurgee" feels he has the confidence to beat this one onslaught, for this one time alone.

Yes, he makes it to the parking lot but has to sit behind the wheel for a few more minutes, lest any slow or sudden upward movement of the buttocks will involuntarily release the mass of you know what from the deep canals of a tunnel less discussed and thought of, the better. Sweat starts to drip from his forehead and his hands get sweaty. He eyes the distance from his lot to the main entrance to the discharge cell. A mere thousand meters; a former athlete, such a distance, a sail in the wind, but not after having gained a few pounds all these years around the belly (part of which is now threatening to unwind and beat the gun, shooting out from the starting blocks without a moment's hesitation).

He has to weigh the possibilities of meeting someone, anyone; could even be his boss wanting to stop for a chat or give instructions. Worst still, the cell could be occupied. Contingencies, the pants need to be discarded. Forget it! No one needs to see him naked below the waist. End of a career.

He opens the door and gets his laptop, cursing the fact that he cannot leave it in the car lest it gets stolen. And now the "Long Walk to Discharge" commences. Old Mandela never had to encounter this. He cannot run as an injury had deprived him of this physical feat. But a slow foxtrot leads him to the cell. The trot that not only works his legs forward but in an uncanny way locks the two folds of his buttocks...... "it's coming, it's coming... God, have mercy on me," he prays.

He walks straight ahead without stopping and responding to the many "Hello, Sir" greetings with a suppressed smile that would only lead to a sudden loss of concentration in keeping the splurge intact within the one way discharge canal.

Finally, he makes it to the cell and one is clear for entry. But it is too late. The door is shut heavily sending tremors across the floor; his belt is stuck and his knees smack each other, trying to control the flow as he squeezes the gates of discharge with a force of his mind; but knows it will not hold the pressure. Pants are discarded and his undies get stuck between his legs. He can see and feel the slime oozing down his legs as he grabs the undies and flings it off, sending a spray of brown, seemingly chocolaty looking discharge all over the side walls of the cell.

A quick drop of the seat and as he rests his bottom and allows a sigh of relief coupled with gushes of watery and oozy release, he slowly examines and contemplates his next move. The pants need to be washed as a tributary had been formed from the main canal. But his undies, now staring at him from the wall, stuck on the flush knob holding clear remnants of discharge as with the walls of the cell. The cleaner will have a hair rising experience and curses accompanied.

All over, he slowly washes the pants. Lucky that they are silky and black as it will not look so noticeable. After a short while, still in the cell, he hears no one else outside. Knowing that the cleaner may walk in at any time, he opens the door and walks out, without a care in the world with no sign of any abnormalities other than the cool feel of his pants and a pungent texture still lingering within. His final decision and resolution; there is a reason for R&Rs. Use them, or another poor soul (not forgetting the cleaner's nightmare) goes through a similar pain of discharge.

Moral of the story.....?

*R&Rs are there for a purpose. When you need to stop and have a break, a short shut eye, hot cup of coffee or if you have to "go" to release your bowels, **just do it**. Do not wait for an invitation because what happens in the end, may not be so pleasant.*

MONTH END FEAST

"Hei guys, heard that Warden has instructed 'Baby' (our hostel cook) to prepare for the month end feast this Saturday," Jacob announced as he walked into Prem's room in the hostel. Prem's room was usually the meeting place for most of the seniors; he being a Super Senior and all that (still doing his B. Com [Bachelor of Commerce] ...his sixth year for a three year course).

"Oh my God, so fast ah? I thought we just had one recently," quipped Ramesh, his roommate. Strangely, he did not sound too enthusiastic about the month end dinner.

"Better you guys be prepared. Heard Baby is preparing his specialty; mutton briyani and Mysore dhal with assorted vegetables and his ever famous UFO chapattis," Jacob continued.

"What UFO Chappatis?" I asked. All responded at the same time, ".... Brother, you definitely don't want to know. But do come and don't say we never warned you."

But none, I was made to understand, were actually looking forward to the dinner based on past experience. And based on past experience, all were reminded to bring along pails filled with water to the dinner, and leave them outside the hall; easily reachable for a quick dash to the "you know where".

I was not really sure what this whole ruckus was about. Incidentally, this was my first month end dinner and was really looking forward to enjoying a good hearty meal.

When Saturday arrived, after the sunset mass, I joined a few of my hostel mates and headed to the Mess. But most of my mates went back to the hostel to change into their "lungies" (sarongs) and reminded me about the pail of water that we needed to bring along to the dinner. Honestly, I was under the impression that they were planning a "water fight" or something to that effect. So I decided neither to bring along a pail nor change as I wanted to be dressed for the occasion.

When I arrived at the Mess Hall, just outside, along the corridor, arranged in a long colourful row, were pails and pails filled with water that resembled a carnival parade.

Inside the Mess Hall, practically all who were there were in their *"lungies"* and though conversation was making quite a din, none looked eager for a hearty meal which I for one, was looking forward to.

Other than me, the only other foreign student, Lim Ah Gua, was also dressed immaculately. And like me, eager to dig into the meal prepared by Baby.

Both Lim and I were first year Pre-university students enrolled in St. Phil's College, Mysore; now having just enrolled for a month. Though not totally impressed with Baby's cooking, we nevertheless ate what was dished out without any complaints. Both of us were however ardent *"Magie Mee"* (Magie noodles) eaters and had packet loads of them which we usually had for most of our dinners, if we decided against heading to the Mess to savour Baby's menu.

When the time for dinner was announced, as usual, Warden Candy would begin with the opening prayers, a short speech and a reminder not to rush to the "unmentionable" and I was wondering why no one was paying any attention to him, but was looking towards the Mess helpers carryings silver food containers, dishing out food on banana leaves spread out on the long tables.

First, there was Briyani – orange in colour, full of raisins and cashew nuts, but a bit too soft for my liking. Then two chapattis each; hard as rocks, and the best part was that it was not placed on the banana leaves as one would normally serve; but flung from a short distance as the servers walked past each of us sitting at the dining table. The chapattis came swirling like UFOs landing precisely on each banana leaf with a "thud". And then in very quick successions, mutton *"perettal"* (dry curry), fried chicken, vegetable *"sambar"* (gravy), one piece of fried fish, two different vegetables and for dessert, a cup of whitish *"payasam"* (vermicelli in sweet milk) and two yellowish balls of *"gulap jamuns"* (deep fried floured balls in sugar syrup). Then silence. Everyone dug heartily into their food.

The spread was tantalisingly spicy and I may admit, delicious though it seemed quite oily to my taste. Only later was I told that Baby usually added a good dosage of Castor Oil, as instructed by the college's Hostel Committee. This was considered the monthly stomach cleansing program practiced as advised by the Health Board of Mysore. And cleanse, it definitely did.

Everyone gorged without a moment's hesitation. Handful of the spicy hot food was quickly devoured, and the only noise to be heard was the munching and gashing of meat and vegetables in the mouths of all present. It was like a race as to who would complete the meal first. The urgency to quicken the completion of this spread in order to engage in a more important task ahead, that needed to be addressed soonest the partaking of the night's dinner came to an end.

Not even halfway through the meal, my stomach suddenly started to churn and as I continued to eat, I could not help wonder whether I should stop and let my stomach take a short break. This was when I slowly took my eyes away from the food and looked up to see the rest of my hostel mates. All had that uneasy stomach-churning look and when I glanced at our Warden, Candy, his food was not touched at all and his only gaze was towards all of us; a smirk as if expecting what he had planned all along with Baby, under the instructions of the hostel's Food Committee. Then, without a word, just like that, he got up and quickly left the Mess Hall.

And then, I heard it. Imagine; the sweet, melodious sound of a far off wind, breaking through the wilderness of sanity, followed closely by a sudden gush and a stench of curried dhal and rotten eggs. And then another, and another and, *"Ooi, stop farting la. Cannot wait until we finish our food?"* But there was no waiting. No holding back on what was already anticipated and expected. No stopping as each of those who were in the midst of completing their food were already rolling up their leaves and standing up, clutching their tummies. Each individual emitting the dreadful smell from their rear. Each cursing the other but silently embracing their own personal aroma as it mingled with the rest creating an inferno of unbearable stench, short of exploding if someone decided to end everyone's misery by just striking a matchstick.

And then it happened. A human stampede like one I have never seen or experienced before in my life. And like the sound of a starter's gun, practically everyone broke wind simultaneously and the smell of pent up gas comprising of an assortment of Indian Banana Leaf food, laced with Castor Oil, exploded with fury adding to the dark ambience of the Mess Hall. Everyone present scrambled towards their individual pails; some took those that were nearest to them, not bothered if it was theirs or someone else's. All were making a quick beeline dash to the unlighted, damp and obnoxious smelling latrines – nine in total, just behind the Mess Hall. Nine latrines to serve 150 hostel mates who had just so many seconds to let go what was now like an avalanche; precariously forming inside their bowels and already gushing down dangerously just reaching the tip of their sphincter before the final discharge.

As for me; I was strangely okay. Stomach? So, so. Just trying to absorb the catastrophe that was unfolding before my very eyes. As for Lim Ah Gua; nowhere to be seen, but I did see an Oriental dash frantically by. He being the only Chinese in the hostel, I suspected it was Ah Gua.

But my control of the bowels was only short lived when I
too felt the surging gust of hot lava already on its way out. I
did not fart like the others, knowing fully well that breaking
wind would create a rear opening which would be enough
for a full discharge to be executed. I was so afraid to even
stand up but I had to go. Garnering all my strength and
using the muscles of my buttocks, I compressed my rear
opening as tightly as I could. One step, two steps and all

along in my mind... *"what do I do for water?"*; knowing fully well that I had decided against bringing a pail of water as advised. *"Get to the lavatory; the rest...belakang kira"* (figure that out later as per Malay language translation), were my only thoughts as I pushed my way towards the already long queue at each respective latrine. I could barely contain myself, and with the sound of anguish followed by sighs of relief coming from each cubicle, I could not take it any longer and just slumped on the cold floor.

Many reading this may be of the opinion that I am just exaggerating and that no one could have experienced what I was going through at that very precise moment. It was like all hell was about to freak out. You need to imagine my situation and for a moment reminisce a similar incident you would definitely have experienced one time or another in a not so distant past.

And yes, I collapsed even as I vaguely heard some of the others shout out, "Dai, give way to this bloody shitty Malaysian da. He is already letting go without even standing in queue like the rest of us."

"Was I where as they said I was?" But sanity was not the order of the day. Neither was it high on the agenda as I practically did a leopard crawl towards the latrine nearest my sight. I could feel feet thumping up and down as I believe many wanted to get clear off my way. But what was this sticky hotness that I was feeling oozing through my pants and ……. that smell! More overpowering than the stench that was already blanketing the whole rear area outside the Mess heading towards the latrines. I crawled and dragged my way, making it to the end of the long queue; leading to the latrines, and from the conversation I heard, they were totally clogged up with shit, as water from each pail was not enough to flush the mess through the outgoing tube.

Note: *Latrines those days were not equipped with a flush system and the only way to make "it" disappear was by pouring buckets of water into the squat bowl.*

But it was to no avail; as I had already messed up, practically defecated in my pants as I could not hold the outflow any longer. In a way, that was good because what I saw the next morning, every latrine was a shit nest where due to the overflow of excreta, the latrine floors were also flooded. Apparently, those who had been standing in the queue had decided to just lift their *"lungies"* and release wherever there was a clean space still available which was a near impossibility.

I remember walking slowly to the wash cubicles where there were already a dozen or so guys, totally naked, scooping water from the water vessels used for bathing; cleansing themselves. They, like me, were not able to contain the hot lava that had oozed out; every bit with

Baby's signature *"dhal* and Castor Oil", indicating the brains behind this mess.

Quick forward........ *"Hei guys,"* I quipped, *"it is on the notice board. Month end feast this Saturday. Do not forget water buckets and wear disposable lungies ya."* I was now an expert. Knowing what to expect and the emergency response required.

Moral of the story.......?

One has to heed to warnings and tell-tale signs lest one is caught "unaware" and ends up the fool of the community one is party to.

Printed in the United States
by Baker & Taylor Publisher Services

Printed in the United States
by Baker & Taylor Publisher Services